The Pink Clip

Cheska Kelly Mae Borja

Ukiyoto Publishing

All global publishing rights are held by

Ukiyoto Publishing

Published in 2024

Content Copyright © Cheska Kelly Mae Borja

ISBN 9789364942812

*All rights reserved.
No part of this publication may be reproduced, transmitted, or stored in a retrieval system, in any form by any means, electronic, mechanical, photocopying, recording or otherwise, without the prior permission of the publisher.*

The moral rights of the authors have been asserted.

This is a work of fiction. Names, characters, businesses, places, events, locales, and incidents are either the products of the author's imagination or used in a fictitious manner. Any resemblance to actual persons, living or dead, or actual events is purely coincidental.

This book is sold subject to the condition that it shall not by way of trade or otherwise, be lent, resold, hired out or otherwise circulated, without the publisher's prior consent, in any form of binding or cover other than that in which it is published.

www.ukiyoto.com

To all those who embrace uniqueness and
courageously pursue their dreams.

Acknowledgements

Writing "The Pink Clip" has been a rewarding journey, made possible by the support and encouragement of many wonderful individuals and organizations.

I extend my heartfelt gratitude to my family and friends for their unwavering support and belief in my writing journey. Your love has been my strength.

Special thanks to Ukiyoto Publishing for believing in my vision and making my dream of publishing "The Pink Clip" a reality. Your professionalism and support throughout the publishing process have been invaluable.

To the readers of "The Pink Clip," thank you for your interest in this story. Your support and curiosity mean the world to me.

To God be all the glory!

Contents

Synopsis	1
It Hurts	2
Reminiscence	5
Awakened	9
Bloody Hands	14
Strange Calm	19
About the Author	*24*

Synopsis

Stephanie, once adored as a princess by her loving parents, finds her world shattered after her father's death and her mother's remarriage. As she grows up, dark secrets and abuse haunt her new family life. Determined to confront the horrors lurking within her home, Stephanie resolves to uncover the truth and put an end to the cycle of torment. The story explores themes of resilience, familial betrayal, and the quest for justice amidst overwhelming adversity.

It Hurts

She's coming.

I can hear her footsteps echoing through the silent house, each step a heavy thud in the stillness of the night. My heart races, knowing what inevitably follows. I bury myself deeper under the covers, hoping against hope that it might shield me from the impending storm.

The door creaks open, a sound that pierces the quiet like a knife. Panic tightens my chest as her voice cuts through the darkness, sharp and unforgiving.

"Oh, God! She's coming." My lips tremble in agony.

"What the hell are you doing, Steffi? Wake up!"

Her words are laced with anger, tearing through the fragile peace of the night.

I pull the blankets over my head, squeezing my eyes shut, trying to block out the reality unfolding around me.

"Damn it, Steffi! I told you to get up!"

Her footsteps draw nearer, the rhythm of her approach like a drumbeat of dread in my ears.

Suddenly, I feel her hand, fingers gripping my hair tightly, pulling with a force that brings tears to my eyes. I refuse to open them, desperately trying to ignore the sharp pain radiating from my scalp. I bite my lip, refusing to give her the satisfaction of seeing me flinch.

"Why do you still wear that clip?! Throw it away!"

Her voice is a mixture of frustration and disappointment, fingers digging into my scalp as she rips the clip from my hair.

I open my eyes, tears already stinging, searching the dimly lit room for the clip now discarded on the floor. It was a small, inconspicuous thing, but to me, it held memories of happier times—of my father's gentle touch and words of comfort.

"How many times have I told you not to wear that fucking clip again? You're so stubborn!"

Her words are a barrage, each one like a hammer blow to my fragile resolve.

Tears stream down my cheeks unchecked, my voice trembling as I speak through the anguish.

"I wish… I wish you weren't my mother. I regret being your daughter. It's the worst thing that's ever happened to me."

Silence fills the room, heavy and suffocating. Then, in one swift motion, her hand connects with the side of my face, the slap ringing in my ears. I collapse to the floor, stunned by the suddenness and force of the blow.

I taste blood in my mouth, a bitter reminder of the pain both physical and emotional. But it's not the sting of the slap or the metallic tang in my mouth that hurts the most—it's the realization that the woman standing over me, so full of anger and disappointment, is someone I no longer recognize.

Clutching the clip in my hand, I hold onto it as if it were a lifeline. It's more than just a hair accessory; it's a symbol of the love and innocence I once knew, now shattered and lost.

She storms out of the room, leaving me curled on the floor, my body shaking with sobs. I press my hand to my cheek, feeling the heat of the mark left behind, a physical reminder of the rupture between us.

Reminiscence

"*Happy Birthday, darling Steffi! Blow your candles.*"

I blew out the candles, my heart swelling with joy as I made my wish. Mommy's warm embrace followed, her arms wrapping around me tightly.

"*I love you, baby! Happy Birthday!*" she whispered in my ear.

Her words, although familiar, felt like a fresh breath of love. She told me she loved me every day, yet it never lost its magic.

Suddenly, I realized something. "*Where's daddy, mommy? Is he coming?*"

"*Of course, baby. Why not? Oh, look! There he is!*" she replied, her voice bright.

I turned and saw daddy approaching. I ran towards him and leaped into his arms.

"*Daddy, you're here!*"

"*Happy Birthday, Princess Steffi. I have a present for you,*" he said, handing me a small box wrapped beautifully.

"Wow! What is it, daddy?" I asked, my excitement bubbling over.

"Open it for daddy."

I tore open the wrapping paper to reveal a stunning white dress and a pink hair clip.

"Wow! These are beautiful, daddy! Thank you so much!"

"Beautiful just like my baby Steff. Wear it now, baby," he said, smiling warmly.

I dashed back to mommy for help. She helped me put on the dress, which fit perfectly. Then, she told me to ask daddy to pin the clip in my hair.

"Daddy, can you pin it for me?"

"Of course!" he said, carefully placing the pink clip in my hair. It complemented my dress perfectly.

"How do I look, daddy?"

"Perfect! My princess is so pretty!"

"Oh yes, I agree!" mommy added, her face glowing with happiness. She set up the camera on a stand.

Daddy picked me up, and mommy stood on my other side, with me sandwiched between them.

I smiled my brightest smile, feeling a warmth and happiness that filled my heart.

camera flashes

The living room was filled with bright balloons and colorful streamers, making it look like a magical wonderland. A table was set up with delicious treats—cupcakes, cookies, and a big bowl of fruit punch. My friends from school were all around, laughing and playing games. There was a piñata shaped like a unicorn hanging in the corner, waiting to be cracked open.

The cake was a masterpiece, a three-tiered wonder adorned with edible flowers and topped with a princess figurine that looked just like me in my new dress. Everyone sang *"Happy Birthday"* as I stood in front of it, feeling like the luckiest girl in the world.

After the cake, we played party games. Pin the tail on the donkey was a big hit, and we all took turns, giggling as we tried to stick the tail in the right spot while blindfolded. Then came the piñata, and with a few good swings, candy rained down, and we all scrambled to gather as much as we could.

Mommy and daddy watched with joy; their smiles wide as they saw how much fun we were having. Every so often, they would catch each other's eyes and share a look that made me feel warm inside. Their happiness was contagious, spreading through the room and making the day even more special.

As the party wound down, daddy brought out the camera again to capture more memories. He took pictures of me with my friends, with mommy, and of course, with him. Each photo was a treasure, a snapshot of a perfect day.

When the last guest had left and the house was quiet again, mommy and daddy sat with me on the couch, looking through the pictures. We laughed at the funny faces and smiled at the sweet moments. They hugged me close, and I felt their love surround me, making me feel safe and cherished.

This birthday, with its laughter, love, and unforgettable moments, was the best day of my life. I hope this will never end.

Awakened

"*Wake up, Steffi. I said don't you ever sleep!*"

I opened my eyes and realized that I was just dreaming. Again.

I wished I didn't wake up.

I really wished I didn't.

Waking up is a nightmare.

My life is a nightmare.

Reality is a nightmare.

My mom is a nightmare.

Except him...

"Sonia! What the hell are you doing?!"

Daddy came rushing into the room.

Dad... Please help…

I couldn't find my voice.

All I could do was cry and cry, and shout silently.

"Are you okay, baby?"

I shook my head as tears started rolling down my cheeks. My eyes were cloudy, my vision blurry.

I'm not okay, daddy. Please help me. Please rescue me.

"How dare you hurt, Stephanie? She's all mine! All mine!"

His voice was inaudible, so I didn't know what he was saying. All I knew was that daddy pulled mommy away from me. He dragged her outside the room.

I wiped the tears away and curled up in a ball.

This wasn't the first-time mommy abused me this way.

I don't understand why. I thought she loved me. But she was always mad at me, especially during nighttime and whenever daddy arrived home from work.

It all started one gloomy night, when the birds were resting and bats were out hunting. Mommy entered the room.

As I approached mommy to give her a kiss and a hug, I was stopped in my tracks.

Mommy looked pale, like she was frightened or angry. I wasn't quite sure. I'd never seen mommy with that face.

I inched slowly towards her and asked in a timid voice, *"What's wrong, mommy?"*

Her eyes flared up, and she grabbed my arm so tight that I cried in agony.

"Mommy, it hurts!"

"Shh. Don't use this."

She removed the pink clip from my hair and threw it away.

"But why, mommy? I like that clip. That was the last present daddy gave to me. I want to treasure this clip forever."

"Just don't use this again. I'll buy you another one."

"No, mommy! I don't want to!"

I shook my head vigorously. I knew mommy would give in to what I wanted.

Because I'm their princess, they would give me everything I wanted.

"Shut up!"

I was in total shock when a slap landed on my right cheek.

"Mo-mommy?"

I couldn't figure out what was happening. This was the very first time that mommy shouted at me and the very first time she ever laid hands on me.

Since then, her supposed to be "goodnight kisses" turned into "nightmares" instead.

Every night became a battlefield. The warmth and comfort of my pink clip was distant memories, overshadowed by the terror that took place in my bedroom. I wish I have here with me my dress that Daddy gave me.

Mommy's face, once so loving, became a mask of anger and frustration. I would lie in bed, clutching my teddy bear, trying to stay as quiet as possible, hoping she wouldn't come in. But she always did.

Her footsteps in the hallway became the sound I dreaded most. Each night, she would storm into my room, her eyes blazing with an intensity that scared me to my core. She would yank me out of bed, shouting words I didn't understand but felt like daggers in my heart.

"Mommy, please!"

I would cry, but my pleas fell on deaf ears. She would slap me, shake me, and throw my favorite toys across the room. The pink clip, my once-treasured gift, lay forgotten in a corner, a symbol of the love that had turned into something monstrous.

Daddy would sometimes intervene, pulling her away and trying to calm her down. But even his presence couldn't erase the fear that had taken root in my heart. I wanted to scream, to run away, to find a place where the nightmares couldn't reach me. But I was trapped.

One evening, after another night of terror, I found myself in front of the mirror, looking at the girl who stared back at me. Her eyes were red and swollen from crying, her cheek still stinging from the latest slap. I touched my face, feeling the pain both inside and out.

"Why, mommy?" I whispered to my reflection. *"Why do you suddenly hate me?"*

There was no answer, only silence. The same silence that filled my room every night after she left, leaving me alone with my tears.

Bloody Hands

12:00 am.

It's July 12th, my 13th birthday.

I know I won't receive any present from my mom but slaps and brutality.

This is it. My Independence Day.

I gazed at my reflection in the mirror before me.

Daddy finds me beautiful, but Mommy doesn't.

Daddy loves me, but Mommy doesn't.

Daddy takes care of me, but Mommy doesn't.

Even though Daddy is not my real father, he always tells me that I am beautiful, precious, and his. Just like my real Daddy, but my real Daddy is long gone. Daddy died in a car accident, and the rest is a painful history. My stepdad is good to me, unlike Mommy. He told me to always think of him as my real Daddy, and I did since then.

Right now, this is the moment I have been waiting for. I made up my mind to proceed with my dreadful plan.

I walked towards my vintage mirror and looked at myself. I threw the mirror and picked up a broken piece. I sliced my finger with it, and blood flowed freely. Funny how I felt no pain, so I figured this would do.

I've planned this for a long time, and now I'm going to do it. No one can stop me. NO ONE!

I walked towards my mom's room. I saw her, lying peacefully under the covers.

How dare she sleep peacefully?!

I inched closer to the edge of the bed. I slowly pointed the sharp piece of the broken mirror at her chest, ready to stab her to death.

"Steffi, what are you doing?"

Oh! She's awake. This monster is awake.

"Hi, Mommy. It's simple. I'm going to stab you little by little until you lose consciousness. Isn't it a great idea?"

"Steffi... No..."

She wrapped her hands over my wrist, but she did not push me away. I smiled wickedly, losing my rationality.

"Will this hurt, Mommy? How about I start by cutting your throat?"

"N-no. Please baby... Listen to me."

"Why should I listen to you?! Did you ever listen to me? Huh! You don't need to worry about your heart because you don't have one! You're cruel, Mom! Very, very cruel! You don't even treat me like your daughter! You're a terrible mother!"

I drove the broken mirror into her chest. Blood splattered onto my face.

"Stephanie! AHHHHH!"

I didn't care about her groans. It was music to my ears. I pushed the sharp object deeper and deeper until her body was a pool of blood.

"You deserve this, evil woman! HAHAHAHA."

I burst out laughing. I couldn't contain the joy in my heart anymore, so I let it out. Even though my hands were cut, I didn't care. All I knew was that this gave me so much happiness, hearing this woman cry in agony.

"Baby, I'll ex-explain everything..."

"Shut up! Why are you not even fighting back! Are you going to kill me too? Go ahead!"

I pulled the mirror out and thrust it into her chest once more. Then I pulled it out and stabbed her again. Over and over.

"Hahaha. Yes! That's it! Scream for your life!"

I shouted and let out my rage. I thrust the shard of mirror repeatedly. I didn't care if her hot blood covered my once innocent hands.

"I am your mom, Steffi. W-why did you do this? I love you."

"You still dare to speak? What a wretched woman!"

I looked at the masterpiece I had created. I could not see even a tiny resemblance of my mother in this woman. She was a total monster!

"Steffi... G-go... Cab-cabinet."

I slapped her face hard. *"Shut up!"*

She stopped moving, and even her breathing ceased. I raised my hands, covered in her hot blood.

I did it... I just killed my worthless, evil mother.

Does this make me a killer?

No! I don't think so. She kills me every day.

My heart filled with laughter and satisfaction.

"What happened here?! Holy shit! Why is Sonia covered in blood?"

It's step-dad!

"Daddy..."

I dropped the broken mirror, and tears filled my eyes. Why am I crying? How dare I feel guilty of killing my evil mother?!

He moved towards me and held my bloody hands.

"It's alright, sweetie. Everything's alright."

He kissed my head and then smiled at me.

I paused for a while and confusion flooded my mind.

Why did he smile? Is he happy I killed Mom?

"I'll be right back. This calls for a celebration. I'll get your clip, okay? So that you will be more beautiful, my baby."

He smirked and left my sight.

I was left there, confused and puzzled. Looking at my mother's warm body, I gazed at the cabinet that she pointed a while ago.

"What's in there? Is there something that I need to know?"

Strange Calm

I slowly approached the cabinet, a strange mix of curiosity and apprehension swirling in my chest. Something about it drew me in, urged me to open it despite the fluttering uncertainty in my stomach.

With trembling hands, I reached for the door, pushing it open to reveal a neatly wrapped box tucked behind my mother's familiar nightgown. The sight of it, adorned with a delicate ribbon, evoked a sense of both familiarity and mystery.

Carefully, I lifted the lid. Inside lay a pristine white dress, its soft fabric unfolding like a memory from a time when things were simpler, when Dad was still here.

It was my dress that Daddy gave me!

Tears welled up as I cradled the dress against my chest, feeling his presence in every stitch, every fold.

"Daddy... I missed you. Wish you were here. But... I just killed mommy. Will you forgive me?"

I whispered, my voice catching with emotion.

Then, my eyes fell upon a letter nestled beneath the dress. With trembling fingers, I unfolded it, my heart pounding louder with each word I read.

"Dearest Stephanie,

Happy Birthday, princess Steffi. It's been so long since I called you that. How I wish I could hug you while you're awake. But I can't, I shouldn't. I can only hug you when you're sleeping because that's the time I can sneak into your room and be with you. Every time I hit you, baby, it pains me more than you know. I also slap myself a hundred times and even curse myself. But I know it won't compare to what you have suffered.

If only your daddy is here. If only he's alive. I'm really sorry, baby. It's all my fault. I should not have married your stepdad and brought him to this home. I should have known, but it's too late now.

But I have a plan. On your birthday, we will escape from this hell. Your psychopath stepdad will no longer harm you. You can now wear your pink clip again. I don't why he's so turned on every time you wear that clip, but today it will end here.

I'm sorry baby, for hurting you. I only did that just so that your stepdad will be disgusted at you and lose his evil libido. Everytime I slap your face, that psychopath satisfies his being, making him leave you and not touch you again. I have lots of things to explain to you baby, so please trust me. Under that white dress of yours, I prepared a gun. Please keep that and I'll find a good chance and kill him myself. He won't be able to lift a finger on my baby Steffi anymore. He won't hurt us anymore. Please be patient, baby. Happy Birthday, baby. I love you forever and always.

Love, Mommy"

The words blurred through my tears, each line a testament to Mom's enduring love and the depths of her sacrifices. My heart pounded as I frantically searched the box for the gun she mentioned, my breath catching in panic when I couldn't find it. Fear gripped me as I sensed someone behind me.

Turning slowly, I faced him—my stepfather, a chilling presence that made my skin crawl. His eyes gleamed with malice as he pressed a cold object against the back of my head.

"Are you looking for this?" he sneered, holding up the gun Mom had hidden for my protection.

I bit my lip, tasting blood, my entire body shaking with a mix of terror and defiance. His laughter echoed in the room, a cruel sound that spurred me to steel myself against the fear.

"Why?"

It was the only word that came out of my mouth. I ruined everything!

"I hate to say this, but our role play is over. Your mommy should have played along with me, but she just has to be stubborn and defy me. That's okay, we can be together now, my bride, forever and always," he taunted, his voice dripping with excitement. He placed the pink clip in my hair, his eyes filled with lust.

"Daddy... Wh-why?" I cried in agony, my tears flowing like a river.

My step-dad burst in laughter and pulled me into his arms. I can feel something hard rubbing against my back as I felt his hot breath hovering my neck.

"Oh my, lovely bride. Steffi, you are really beautiful."

I heard him moaned over my ear as I feel his hands caressing my fragile, little body. I quivered under his touch as I sense the disgust filling my lungs.

I pulled something out from my pocket--- it was the bloody mirror shard that I used to kill my mom. I took a deep breath and a defiant smile quivered on my lips, a silent promise to Mom and Dad, a resolve to face whatever came next with courage.

"See you, Mom and Dad," I murmured softly, steeling myself for the inevitable. With a trembling hand, I repeatedly plunged the mirror shard into my chest, each thrust bringing a wave of searing pain that I forced myself to ignore. The anguish was

overwhelming, but my resolve remained unbroken as I carried out my final act.

"Steffi, no! Stop it right now!"

I can hear his voice resounding in my ears as I collapsed to his arms.

In that fleeting second, amidst the chaos and danger, I found a strange calm—a belief that somehow, beyond this darkness, I would reunite with my parents again.

About the Author

Cheska Kelly Mae Borja

Cheska, a quiet and introspective girl, has been crafting stories since her high school days. She dreams of publishing her own book one day, with the hope of holding a beautifully bound copy of her work in her hands. Her inspirations are varied and vibrant, drawn from the people she encounters, the intricacies of their lives, and the emotions evoked by the music she loves. Whether it's a fleeting moment with a stranger or a haunting melody, these experiences fuel her creativity and deepen her desire to share her stories with the world.

www.ingramcontent.com/pod-product-compliance
Lightning Source LLC
LaVergne TN
LVHW041643070526
838199LV00053B/3529